Night Shift

D.L. Winchester

Winchester Horror Publishing

Copyright © 2026 by D.L. Winchester

All rights reserved.

Paperback ISBN: 979-8-9942426-2-9
eBook ISBN: 979-8-9942426-3-6

No part of this publication may be reproduced, distributed, or transmitted in any form or by any means, including photocopying, recording, or other electronic or mechanical methods, without the prior written permission of the publisher, except as permitted by U.S. copyright law. For permission requests, contact Winchester Horror Publishing.

The story, all names, characters, and incidents portrayed in this production are fictitious. No identification with actual persons (living or deceased), places, buildings, and products is intended or should be inferred.

Book Cover by Christy Aldridge at Grim Poppy Designs

First edition 2026.

For the folks working the Graveyard Shift.
I hope your night goes better than Trey's.

1

I PULLED MY PICKUP truck into the gas station on Route 209. Parking at the pump, I got out and headed inside.

"Hey, Trey," the owner greeted me. Eddie had worked there since before I was born. His dad had built the station, and now it was Eddie's. Who knew what would happen when Eddie retired? His kids had left the area long ago and wouldn't move back, not even to keep the family tradition alive.

"What's up?" I asked, grabbing a bag of chips off the rack and heading for the cooler.

"Same old same old," Eddie replied. "You got big plans tonight?"

"New job," I said, walking back toward the register. "Night shift at the Carlton Factory."

Eddie shook his head. "All I hear about that place is bad."

I shrugged. "It's been three months since the mine closed. They're the last place I applied, but the only one to hire me."

"Reckon everyone had that problem. You hear what happened to Wes King?"

I hadn't. Knew him, though. Wes had been one of the managers at the mine, but he'd worked on a different shift from me.

"Lost his pension two years before retirement. Now he's working the loading dock down at the co-op."

"Shit. A lotta folks that had already retired had to go back to work," I replied. The mine had borrowed from the pension fund, trying to stay afloat, but the pension money ran out before the mine recovered, leaving the miners with no jobs, and the retirees with no money.

"At least you're still young. You got time to figure things out. They ever decide if they're gonna press charges?" Eddie took my chips and drink and scanned them.

"State ain't decided shit," I hissed. "Apparently the Attorney General's looking into it, but hell, Representative Wilson made more from the mine than we did." I pulled out my wallet and handed my last five dollar bill across the counter.

Eddie looked at it, then shook his head. "I got this for you, Trey."

"Eddie, I ain't looking for no charity." I felt my face flush as the bill hung in my hand.

"It ain't charity. It's a congratulations for the new job."

I nodded, returning the bill to my wallet before picking up the items.

"Thanks," I muttered. It was charity, and we both knew it, but the way things were in our valley of the Appalachians, I couldn't accept it unless it was dressed up as something different. Hell, it was probably that way in any part of Appalachia.

I went out to the pump and used my credit card to fill the truck's gas tank. That'd be the last purchase I could put on this card, I knew. This new job wasn't gonna change my life, but hopefully it'd be enough to keep the debt collectors away until I could find something that paid decent.

***

The Carlton Factory was almost at the county line, on the main highway. To get there, I had to pass the old mine, sitting silently in the fading daylight.

For the last year, we'd waited, hoping the money wouldn't run out, that someone would come in and buy out the owners. But salvation never came. The mine had closed, sending over a hundred miners into a job market that was already struggling.

I turned off Route 209 onto the four-lane, then a mile or so later, into the parking lot at Carlton. It was a small factory, a metal building with a smaller brick office in front of it.

Looking at it, I almost wanted to cry. Was this what I'd been reduced to? $11.25 an hour, with benefits after ninety days? Not even a third of what I made underground, not counting the benefits.

"Don't worry, it's just temporary," I told myself as I put the chips and drink in my cooler.

Sure. Temporary enough your wife's offering to end her maternity leave early.

That hurt. Elise was a sweetheart to offer, and the elementary school would love to have her back. But she was supposed to have another month to recuperate and bond with Hannah.

It made me feel like less of a man to even consider cutting that short.

So here I was at the Carlton Factory.

I sighed, then opened my car door to get out.

2

THE SUPERVISOR WAS WAITING for me in the lobby. It was sparsely furnished, the company's real name and logo on one of the walls.

It'd been years since the Carlton Company owned the factory, but the name had stuck, like most names around here do.

"Well," he said, looking me up and down. "Another out-of-work miner."

I nodded, trying not to let my irritation show. It was hard to feel judged by someone who showed up to work in a t-shirt and jeans, when I'd left my previous job exhausted and covered in coal dust.

"I done told the office not to hire any more of you. Since the mine closed, they've hired six former miners. None of 'em lasted a month." He shook his head. "This ain't gonna be no cushy union job like you're used to. If that's what you're expectin', you might as well go ahead and go."

I almost did, but the thought of Elise and Hannah stopped me. "The mine wasn't union," I said. "I'm used to working as hard as the next man."

"Ha!" He stuck out his hand. "I'm Tom Stone." I shook his hand, squeezing a little harder than I had to.

He didn't seem to notice.

"You a Kentucky fan?" he asked, pointing to his t-shirt. "I'm ready for basketball season, let me tell you."

Tom was gonna be more talk than work, I could already tell. "Can't say I am."

He narrowed his brow. "Don't tell me. Louisville?"

"Don't watch much basketball," I admitted. "If anything, I'm a Railsplitter fan. My mom and my wife went to school in Harrogate."

"Jesus," he muttered. "Ain't ever heard of a *Railsplitter* fan."

Basketball was religion in our small town. We were firmly in Kentucky Wildcat country. I'd never been all that interested in sports, so claiming my wife's Alma mater was usually enough to change the subject.

But not with my new boss.

"Don't worry," he said, leading me toward the break room. "If you last, you'll come around. Hell, I see my workers more when I play the games on my office TV than any other time."

"Maybe," I agreed.

"Millie will be training you." He pointed to an older woman with straight gray hair. She looked up at me and it felt like someone dropped a brick in my gut.

"Hello, Trey," she said.

"Hi, Mrs. Keene," I replied.

"You two know each other?" Tom asked.

Millie smiled. "Oh yes. Trey and my family go way back."

"Excellent! That's always a good sign."

I forced a smile. "How is Bonnie?"

"You'll see her tonight," Millie replied.

Fuck. Fuck fuck fuck. Bonnie had been my high school girlfriend. It hadn't ended particularly well, and the way Millie was looking at me—like a cat looks at a bird with its feet glued to the ground—I wasn't sure what Bonnie had told her, and how much it had been embellished.

"Good!" Tom clapped me on the back. "Looks like you're already one of the family. Maybe you'll make it after all."

"I'll do my best to get him trained," Millie promised.

"Excellent. I'll leave him in your capable hands." He walked toward the production floor.

I took the seat across the table from Millie. As soon as Tom was out of the room, she reached out and slapped me.

My hand flew to my cheek, probing the stinging skin. "What the hell was that for?"

"That's for breaking Bonnie's heart, you stupid git. Y'all were together for six years, and you up and ended it because Dave drinks a little more than you'd like?"

Someone else walked in, and she lowered her voice. "You just thought you were too good for us after you got a job at the mine. Leave us white trash behind, find an *educated* woman to marry."

"That ain't what happened," I protested.

"Bonnie said it was. You calling her a liar?" Millie challenged.

I paused. It was damn obvious Bonnie was a liar. But I'd spent the past five years doing everything I could to avoid her and her family, so they'd never heard my side of the story. Still, I had to spend the next eight hours with Millie, and the wrong answer here could make that feel like an eternity.

"Maybe I remember it differently," I said, trying to compromise.

Millie wasn't having it. "So why did you break up with Bonnie?"

"That's personal, Mom."

I turned around and saw Bonnie standing behind me, her hands on her hips. "What are you doing here, you sorry son-of-a-bitch? Decide to come crawling back now that the mine closed?"

"No," I said. "Just looking for work, any work. I got a family to support."

Bonnie snorted. "I figured that fancy bitch you married would have run off instead of deigning to endure poverty."

"Elise ain't fancy," I replied. "She's a good woman."

Bonnie shook her head. "Whatever she is, she ain't got no taste."

A bell rang, and I looked up to see the clock on the wall showing nine. "You two will have to finish this discussion later," Millie said. "It's time to go to work."

3

The factory was a small one, turning out custom bubble wrap and other plastic packaging. Rolls of sheet plastic came in one end of the building, ran through the machines, and left as rolls of whatever was being made.

"Hope you like being busy," Millie said. "Ain't no sitting on your ass here."

"Sounds good," I replied.

"These machines ain't like what you're used to," she continued. "You ain't careful, you'll lose a body part or something."

I kept my mouth shut. Working in the mine was plenty dangerous, but I didn't feel like discussing the finer points of roof falls and coal dust.

"We got four machines here. Once you're trained up, you'll run one, from start to finish. Tonight, you'll help me." She grinned. "I'mma make you regret what you did to Bonnie. We'll see how much you can take."

I thought about Elise and Hannah, and the red numbers on my bank statement. "Bring it on," I replied.

★★★

Millie wasn't lying.

The machines were just big enough to be a pain in the ass, having to walk from one end to the other. The control station was small and cramped, leaving me closer to Millie and the stink of cigarette smoke than I wanted to be.

"So if you're gonna call my daughter a liar, what's the truth?" she asked after I came back from rethreading the plastic sheet into the initial rollers. The damn thing was constantly tearing, something Millie put down to "that cheap-ass biodegradable shit."

"Never said she lied, said we just remembered it differently," I deflected, hoping to change the subject.

She laughed. "Boy, that ain't what the look on your face said. So fess up, and I might be a little nicer to ya."

I sighed. It was going to sound stupid. *I* still thought the reasons were stupid. But I didn't regret the break-up. So why not be honest?

"It was two things," I said. "She took up smoking."

Millie's eyes widened. "You broke up because she got herself a vice? Good God. Life's hard enough around here without something to take the edge off."

"Never said it wasn't," I replied. "I just couldn't handle the smell."

She shook her head. "Goddamn coal miner don't like the way cigarettes smell. You're getting the black lung either way. Might as well have some nicotine to take the edge off."

I shrugged. Black lung was a threat, a disease caused by continued exposure to coal dust that wreaked havoc on the lungs of mine workers. While Millie had a point, I hadn't seen fit to help it along with cigarettes. Three months after leaving the mine, I was breathing better than I had in years.

"Anyway, you said there were two reasons," Millie continued.

"The tattoo."

Her jaw dropped. "The tattoo?"

I nodded. Bonnie had gotten a tattoo between her breasts, a bouquet of flowers with my name on a ribbon wrapped around them. "Yeah. Chest tattoos are a huge turn-off for me."

"Did you tell her that?" Millie asked.

"Yep. More than once before she got it."

Millie rolled her eyes. "What the fuck was she thinking?"

I shrugged, remembering the night of our break-up. We'd gone to bed, Bonnie had initiated things, she'd pulled off her shirt, and it was over. As soon as I saw the tattoo, my dick went limp. The next morning, I'd moved out of our trailer.

"You ain't out of the woods, bucko," Millie said. "You still broke Bonnie's heart, and I still hate you for it. But how fucking stupid do you have to be to do the damn thing your man tells you not to do?"

"Attention all employees," a speaker cackled to life.

"Shit," Millie said. "I didn't know that old PA system still worked."

"Attention all employees," it repeated. "Please report to the break room immediately."

4

A FEW MINUTES LATER, seven of us were sitting in the break room: the four operators, a forklift driver, a maintenance guy, and Tom.

The only operator I hadn't met was Kayce. I knew who she was though, as was common in small towns. She'd been a couple years ahead of me in high school, had gotten pregnant by her high school boyfriend, who joined the Marines to get out of Pine Valley. A few months later, he'd called Kayce to tell her he was breaking up with her. Now she was a single mom. Her kid had been one of Elise's students this year. She was plain, brown hair pulled back in a ponytail, wearing a sweatshirt and jeans.

I also knew the forklift driver, Lon Hayes. I'd gone to high school with his son, Dylan. If Lon wasn't balding, I might have thought he was Dylan—dark haired, short, and stocky. On weekends, Lon was the preacher for the Church of Christ. They'd always been the smallest church in the valley, so Lon was bi-vocational. Dylan turned eighteen and got devout, so I slowly stopped spending time with him, and hadn't talked to Lon much since then.

The only one I wasn't familiar with was the maintenance guy. He was about as old as Lon, with "Cooter" stitched on his shirt. He was tall and lanky, with a receding hairline. I'd seen him working on the line next to ours. He seemed competent, at best. I figured he drove in from Harlan, the nearest town of any size.

Seven boxes were on the table. They hadn't been there when we left the break room earlier, I was sure of it. There was also a computer screen on one of the tables, and a pair of cameras mounted in the corners, red lights blinking.

"What the fuck is all this shit?" Tom asked, gesturing at the boxes.

"It ain't mine," Cooter said, crossing his arms.

"Mine either," Kayce said, taking a seat. Bonnie leaned against the wall, glaring at me like this was all my doing.

"Who called us in here?" Lon asked.

Tom shrugged. "It wasn't me. I came to figure out what the hell's going on."

"I didn't even know those speakers still worked," Millie added.

Across from us, the black screen changed to an image of a man I'd seen in town, but didn't know well. "I fixed the speakers," he said.

Everyone looked at the monitor. "Zach Davis," Millie breathed.

"What the fuck is this?" Tom demanded.

"Who's he?" I whispered to Millie.

"He used to be the IT guy here," she whispered back. "They fired him last week."

On the screen, Zach was grinning at us.

"I said, what the fuck are you doing?" Tom demanded again.

"Did you ever hear the one about 'vengeance is mine, says the Lord?'" Zach asked.

Lon nodded. Tom shook his head.

"Well tonight, I am his instrument," Zach announced.

"You can't be serious," Tom said.

"Oh, I am."

"Fuck this." Tom turned to us. "Get back to work. I'll figure out how to disconnect this little creep."

"I wouldn't do that," Zach said in a sing-song voice. "It could have explosive consequences."

The sound of an explosion filled the room, but I couldn't tell if it came from the speakers, or if Zach had actually blown something up. We all looked back at the screen.

"What the hell?" Bonnie asked.

"Well, working wouldn't be too bad," Zach said with a grin. "But when you try to leave…" He pantomimed an explosion. "All the doors are covered. You have to earn your way out."

"Jesus," I muttered, as Kayce began to cry.

"How do we earn our way out, you little cretin?" Millie asked.

"By proving you deserve to live, of course." Zach smiled. "I see none of you have opened my presents yet. Go ahead. There's one for each of you."

"Why should we?" Tom demanded.

"Because it's part of the game," Zach replied. "If you don't play my game, you don't deserve to live."

"Why are you doing this?" Lon asked as Tom passed a box to each of us.

"Because I know what you did. What all of you did. Bonnie and Kayce rejected me. Millie and Cooter talked shit about me. Lon protected Bonnie and Kayce from me. Tom got me fired. And I didn't want the new guy to feel left out."

I took the box from Tom and paused. If I opened it, I'd have to play this freak's games. It was a line I wasn't sure I wanted to cross. I looked at the screen. Zach's eyes weren't directed at me, but I could feel him watching, letting the tension grow. Was he as dangerous as he seemed, or was this all for show?

Then I remembered the explosion, and decided he might be capable of the violence he promised. I pulled open the box.

Inside was a harness, with a hard plastic object in the center. There was a beeping light on the front, along with a bright number 5. It reminded me of a laser tag rig, without the gun.

"Put them on, put them on," Zach said, grinning.

"And if we don't?" Bonnie asked. "We blow up when we step outside?"

"No, I just have to persuade you to play my little game," Zach said.

The image on the screen switched, and I recognized the trailer I'd shared with Bonnie. "I hear you're a dog lover. One push of a button, and no more puppies…"

Bonnie gasped as a series of images cycled across the screen, of homes, including mine. It was almost unbelievable what this fucker had managed to do. Cameras on our houses, information pulled from the systems, how had he prepared this in the week since they'd fired him?

No matter how he'd done it, the threat was clear. We pulled on the vests.

"What is this thing, anyway?" Kayce asked.

"We're going to have some fun tonight. But be careful—if you lose my games, you'll be eliminated." The screen switched again, to a shot of one of the vests strapped to a large pumpkin. A moment later, the vest exploded.

5

We all looked at each other.

"Elimination devices?" Kayce mouthed, running her shaking fingers along the straps.

"And now that you've buckled them, there's a completed circuit. Cut that circuit, and BOOM!" Zach clapped his hands in delight. "Even the new guy put his on! I didn't even have to mention that I'm still in the company computer system and know about his wife, Elise, and his daughter, Hannah."

A wave of anger surged through me. "You keep your hands off them!" I growled.

"Oh, I will, as long as you play my little games. You might even make it home to see them again. I should also mention those vests have a proximity trigger. Even if you manage to escape, if you get too far from the factory, BOOM!"

"Alright, Zach," Lon said, stepping to the front. "What's the game?"

"Games, Lon, *games*!" Zach rubbed his hands together. "I have a full night of fun planned for y'all. But first, I want to prove I'm serious. I wouldn't want you thinking I won't kill you. So we're going to put it to a vote. Who should be the first to die?"

I noticed Tom had his phone out, but whatever he was trying to do wasn't working. "Shit," he mumbled under his breath.

"I did mention I jammed your cell phones, didn't I, Tom?" Zach taunted. "Now, to vote. Who will be the first to die?"

"You can't do this!" Kayce said.

"I can, and I am." Zach grinned, leaning back in his chair. "Since you spoke up, keep talking. Who's your vote, Kayce?"

She looked around, tears filling her eyes again. Finally, she whispered, "Tom."

"Oho! The boss is on the board! Cooter, you're next!"

"Tom," he said, avoiding looking at Tom.

"Damn," Zach said. "This election may be boring. Bonnie?"

"Trey," she said, looking at me.

I felt my stomach drop. She had every reason to hate me, but in a matter of life or death, I hoped she'd put it aside.

"Bonnie doesn't like the new guy!" Zach crowed. "I wanna hear this story!"

Bonnie shrugged. "He broke my heart. Fuck him."

"Damn, that's cold," Zach replied. "Millie, what's your vote?"

"Trey," she said without even looking at me. I'd hoped after our talk earlier, things might have been different, but apparently not.

My face must have been downcast, because Zach started laughing. "Poor guy. She wasn't gonna vote for Tom. She's fucking him!"

"What?" Bonnie yelled, looking between her mother and the supervisor.

"That's right, Sweetie," Zach taunted. "You're not the only one getting some from the boss."

"You son of a bitch!" Bonnie yelled, turning to face Tom. "My *mom?*"

He shrugged. "Your pussy ain't special. I see why Trey left your ass."

Bonnie's mouth fell open. Millie's face was red, maybe from embarrassment.

Bonnie took a step toward Tom and slapped him. "You wouldn't know good pussy anyway, with that tiny cock of yours!"

"Shit!" Cooter said, laughing. "That explains a lot!"

Bonnie turned. "Don't you fucking start…"

"I think that's enough," Zack cut in, turning our attention back to the screen. "Tom, your vote?"

"Trey," he said, not even looking at me.

"And new guy moves into the lead. Must be nice, to be so popular on your first day. Lon, you're up."

"Lon," he said.

"You're voting for yourself?" Zach asked.

A nod.

"How noble."

"Everyone should have voted for me," Lon replied. "I know where I'm going, and I'm not afraid."

"Too bad, no changing your vote now. I'm sure some people might take you up on that," Zach replied. "Which brings us to our last voter, the one and only New Guy. Will you be like Lon and fall on your sword? Maybe get a little payback on an ex? I can't wait to find out."

There really wasn't a choice. To have any chance of survival, I had to pick Tom. As much as I didn't want to condemn someone else, I also couldn't bear to leave Elise and Hannah. I didn't know what would happen in the event of a tie, but I knew exactly what would happen if I lost.

I took a deep breath. "Tom."

6

For a moment, no one spoke. Then Zach laughed.

"We've got a tie," he announced. "So what should I do? Should I kill both of you?"

God, I hoped he wouldn't. I didn't want to beg, but I didn't want to die either. Elise and Hannah, alone in the world with this cretin. It was something I didn't want to consider. Would he go after them?

Torture them, the way he was torturing me?

"Kill me," Lon said, interrupting my thoughts. "You get your dead man, and neither of these men has to die."

Zach shook his head. "Lon, I ain't through with you yet. No sir." He smiled into the camera. "I think I'll pass the tiebreaking vote." It bugged me how I could feel him looking at me through the screen. "New Guy is wearing a red shirt, which means he's expendable." The camera shifted downward, revealing Zach was wearing a Star Trek shirt. "Still, he's never done me wrong, while Tom, on the other hand…"

"Shut up and do something!" Tom barked.

Zach laughed. "Alright, if you insist.

He pressed a button on his keyboard. Everyone turned to stare at Tom and I. This was it. The moment of truth.

For what felt like an eternity, nothing happened. I wanted to move, to run, to strip off the vest and escape from this goddamned nightmare. But my body refused to respond, the fear managing to make me manic and paralyze me at the same time.

Then the device on Tom's chest jumped out. I heard him exhale, then saw a bloody splotch appear on his shirt. It expanded slowly. Tom looked down at it, then up at us.

"Fuck," he said. "That hurt."

Then he collapsed to the floor.

Lon moved toward him.

"Stop!" Zach barked.

"He needs help!" Lon protested.

"No, he doesn't," Zach snapped. "He lost the vote, he dies."

"Help me, it hurts," Tom moaned from the floor.

"Jesus," Cooter muttered.

Looking at Tom and the damage done, I figured the devices on our chests were like shotgun shells. When they went off, they drove metal balls of some kind into our bodies. Mine was roughly over my heart, which meant a quick death, but Tom had worn his lower.

So his counted as a miss.

A gutshot.

Blood was pooling around Tom, and he was moaning now, weakly. With a final gasp, he went still.

Millie and Bonnie were holding each other, crying. Cooter and Kayce were just staring at Tom's body, looking numb. Lon was staring at Zach, shaking his head.

"You didn't have to do that," he said quietly.

Zach laughed. "Of course not. But he deserved it. And I wanted to. So I did."

"You're a monster," Bonnie said, stepping away from her mother and approaching the screen. "You just killed a man!"

"And he's just the first," Zach replied. "The question y'all should be asking isn't 'Why?' It's 'who's next?'"

His words were chilling. Tom was dead. But this asshole wasn't done. There were six of us left. How many would survive the night?

"Just take me," Lon said. "Let everyone else go, and you can do whatever sick, twisted things you want to me. These folks don't deserve to deal with you. They're good people."

Zach laughed. "Nice try. But no." He smiled. "Good news, boys. You get to sit out the next round. This game's for the ladies."

"Oh, God," Kayce muttered.

Cooter sat down at one of the tables. I felt relieved, but ashamed. I was safe for the moment, but it was because someone else was at risk.

"It's ladies night at the factory," Zach continued. "And the girls are going to put on a little show for us." I heard him pressing buttons on his keyboard. "You can take your vests off, ladies."

For a moment, no one moved. Then Kayce unclipped her vest, shrugging out of it.

"That feels so much better," she said, dropping it on a nearby table. Millie and Bonnie, seeing her survive, quickly followed suit, removing their vests.

"That's a good start," Zach said. "Bonnie, do you remember what you said when I asked you out?"

Bonnie froze.

"Come on, don't be shy. Everyone in the factory heard you the first time."

"Not even if you were the last man on earth," she whispered.

"Exactly!" Zach shook his head. "Kayce, you were nicer, weren't you?"

A nod. "I told you I had a lot going on in my life, and didn't have room for a man."

"And you weren't lying," Zach acknowledged. "You weren't holding out on me because you were fucking your supervisor, may he rot in hell."

A few sets of eyes glanced at Tom's body when he said this.

"So," Zach said, "to celebrate ladies night, we're going to have a strip-off. The one that turns me on the least will die."

7

Lon shook his head. "The hell you're going to do that! I've had about enough of this!"

He stomped toward the camera at the far end of the room, carefully stepping around Tom's body.

"Lon, if you touch that camera, you die," Zach warned.

Lon spun around. "You think you can play God, you little creep? Try to make everyone dance to your tune? Well, I've had enough. No matter what you do, you're going to hell, and I, for one, hope you make the trip sooner rather than later! Until then, I'm going to do everything I can to be a pain in your ass!"

He turned around and reached for the camera.

The sound of the device going off made us jump. Lon's had been positioned well. He fell to the ground immediately, landing on his back, not moving. The hole was in his chest, right over his heart.

On the screen, Zach shook his head. "That was stupid," he announced.

Cooter and I looked at each other. He shrugged. I didn't care if this freak wanted the women to strip down. Zach could look, but he couldn't touch. I'd already seen one of them naked. Seeing two more and staying alive was the preferred option.

"Alright, let's get some music and get this show on the road." A booming bro-country track about country girls blared over the screen's speakers. "Let's start with Bonnie!"

Bonnie hesitated for a moment, looking around the room. Then she got to her feet and walked toward the screen. I looked away. I'd seen her naked plenty of times, and didn't care to do it again.

"Hang on," I heard Zach say. "New Guy isn't looking."

I peeked at the monitor. "Dude, this is for your benefit, not mine. Ain't nobody here I want to see naked."

Zach laughed. "You never know, New Guy." The picture of my house appeared on the monitor. "Maybe you'll be looking for a new woman soon."

My mouth went dry as I stared at the screen. "Don't…" I stammered.

"Then watch the damn show. I went to a lot of effort to bring you this entertainment." Zach's face appeared, and he winked at Bonnie. "Go ahead. Let's see why New Guy left your ass."

Bonnie rolled her eyes. Grabbing the hem of her shirt, she lifted it over her head, revealing a gray sports bra.

"No sexy underwear?" Zach shook his head. "Come on, baby. You gotta do better than that."

Bonnie flipped him off, then slid her jeans down. Turning, she slapped her ass, then dropped her white briefs to the floor.

"Nice ass, baby," Zach encouraged. "Now show me those tits!"

She pulled her bra over her head, freeing her breasts.

Not much had changed from the last time I saw her naked. Bonnie had always been on the petite side, her breasts small handfuls. The tattoo was still there, but I noticed the ribbon with my name had been colored in.

"Goddamn," Zach crowed. "New Guy, how could you give that up?"

I shrugged. "I ain't a big fan of chest tattoos."

"Your loss," Zach said, grinning as Bonnie leaned into the monitor. I wondered what she was doing, until I noticed there was a camera attached. That's where the show was focused.

"Alright, Bonnie, have a seat," Zach told her. She bent over to reach for her clothes. "No! Leave those there. I like you better naked."

Bonnie froze, looking at Cooter, then at me. I shrugged, trying to tell her it didn't matter, I had other things on my mind. She turned and stomped to a seat.

Millie!" Zach called. "You're up!"

Millie stepped in front of the camera and dropped her pants. Stepping out, she lifted her shirt to show a red thong. "You want some of this?"

"God, no," Zach said. "Was Tom blind or something?"

Millie peeled her shirt off, revealing a red bra that matched her thong.

"Mama, I wish you'd taught your daughter better," Zach said. "That's how a woman should dress!"

"It's itchy as hell," Bonnie said.

Zach laughed as Millie removed her underwear, turning slowly for the camera.

Millie didn't look bad for her age. She had a little more weight on her than Bonnie, and a few extra wrinkles, but she'd aged well.

Probably all the damn chemicals in her cigarettes preserving her.

I closed my eyes. I hadn't meant to think that, not about a woman exposing her body to try to save her life. Before Zach realized I wasn't looking, I opened my eyes and looked back at Millie.

"Alright. I'm gonna go pour bleach in my eyes," Zach said, shaking his head.

"Apparently Millie is not a MILF. But that leaves us with Kayce! Come on up, girl!"

She walked up, bent in front of the camera, and pulled the neck of her shirt down. "You want a better look at these?" Her voice had dropped to a husky rasp.

On the screen, Zach nodded. "Oh yes, oh yeah."

Kayce turned around, gyrating her ass as she lifted her shirt over her head, giving us a clear view of her breasts stuffed into a black bra. I actually felt myself growing hard—she looked good, but the things she was doing were enhancing her assets.

She's stripping for her life!
And doing a damn good job!

She turned back around, whipping her hair over her head to hide her tits from the camera. Then she tossed it back, unbuckling her jeans and letting them fall, revealing her matching black underwear.

I thought about my wife, at home, unaware that if I didn't watch this beautiful woman undress, her life would end, along with our daughter's.

The sound of a smack brought me back to the show. Kayce had slapped her ass, drawing a hoot from Zach and an appreciative eye raise from Cooter. She dropped her panties next, and stepped out of them. Kayce was bigger than Bonnie, full-bodied, but she was moving better than Bonnie had. She shook her ass for the camera, then reached behind her and unhooked her bra.

A few seconds passed as Kayce let the anticipation build for Zach, but we had the full view, her free breasts bouncing as she moved. Finally, she turned and smiled at Zach.

"Was this what you wanted to see?" she purred.

"Where the fuck did that come from?" Cooter muttered. "I don't think I've ever heard her say two words."

I shrugged, wondering if I could stop looking now.

"Damn," Zach said. "Okay, ladies, put your vests back on, but only your vests. It's time to find out who's gonna die."

8

Millie stared at the screen for a moment. "What if we don't put our vests back on?"

"Mom, don't," Bonnie said, snapping hers on.

"No." Millie threw her vest to the floor. "What can this creep do to us without these fucking things?"

Kayce had frozen, her hands on the buckles that would complete the circuit and activate her vest. She was watching Millie, standing naked and defiant in front of the screen. Then she shook her head, and buckled her vest.

"You think you're untouchable without the vest?" Zach asked, a smile on his face.

"I don't see how you can get me from behind your screen, you little creep," Millie shot back.

Zach shook his head. "What you don't understand is that it doesn't have to be me. Cooter," he said, looking toward him.

"Yeah?"

"Kill Millie."

He looked down at his hands, then at the table, then back up at Zach. "How? I don't have a weapon."

Zach smiled. "I'm sure you have something in your shop you can use."

Cooter nodded. "Yeah. I do, I guess."

"Go get it," Zach ordered.

He got up without looking at Millie and walked to the door. While he went to get whatever he decided to use, we sat in silence, looking at each other, trying not to look at Millie or the screen.

Seconds dragged into minutes.

Finally, the door swung open, and Cooter stepped inside.

"What did you bring?" Zach asked.

Cooter held up a hammer.

"Crude, but effective," Zach said with a nod. "Kill the bitch."

Cooter paused for a moment.

"Cooter, don't," Bonnie said quietly.

"Don't listen to her, Cooter," Zach said. "You won't survive if you do."

He nodded. "I'm sorry," he whispered to Bonnie. Then he walked toward Millie.

She looked up at him. "I never liked you, asshole. I saw the shit you had on your computer. Fucking pervert!"

Cooter swung the hammer, coming in from the side and smashing the face into Millie's temple. Her skull cracked with an audible *snap,* making me turn my head briefly.

But only briefly. Somehow, I felt like I had a duty to watch these deaths, to witness the brutality these folks were suffering at the hands of a madman.

A brutality I had been close to suffering myself. Hell, it could still happen. The night wasn't over.

Bonnie screamed and stepped toward him, like she was going to stop him, but Kayce grabbed her vest and held her back.

"No. It's not worth it," she whispered.

"That's my mama!" Bonnie yelled as Cooter swung the hammer again. "Don't! Stop!"

Millie fell onto the table, her torso draped across it. The hammer rose and fell, Cooter slamming it into Millie's head again and again, droplets of blood flying across the room with every motion.

Bonnie had collapsed to the floor, sobbing. Kayce tried to put her arms around her, but Bonnie shoved her away.

"You son-of-a-bitch!" she yelled as Cooter raised the hammer and brought it down. The face sank into her skull, leaving only the tip of the claw and the handle sticking out.

Cooter turned toward Bonnie. "Ain't personal. I want to live as much as you do."

"You asshole!" She pushed him out of the way, and threw herself on top of her mother's body. "Mama, sweet mama," she sobbed.

"And then there were four," Zach crowed from the computer screen.

"You son of a bitch!" Bonnie yelled, standing up to face the camera. Her mother's blood covered the front of her body.

Kayce came over and sat down next to me. "You okay?" I asked.

She shrugged. "I just want to get home to my kid."

"Is that why you gave him a show?"

She actually chuckled. "After Baxter left, it took me a few months to sort out the child support situation. My parents had kicked me out, and I didn't have anyone to take care of Riley. But guys on the internet would pay to see me take my clothes off. It got me through."

I nodded. "I hate he treated you like that."

Kayce nodded. "It's tough on Riley. He's old enough now to understand he ain't got a dad. He can't lose me too."

I nodded my understanding as Bonnie collapsed back on top of her mother's body, her argument with Zach concluded.

"Alright, folks," Zach said. "Our next game is a treasure hunt. Somewhere in the plant, I've hidden one of these," he held up a metal smiley-face keychain. "Find it, and you won't have to participate in the next round."

9

Bonnie stood again, her body even bloodier than before. "You bastard," she yelled, pointing at the screen. "You sick, twisted bastard! None of us will make it out alive! None of us! Just kill us now instead of fucking with us!"

"No!" Kayce yelled, jumping to her feet. "I've got to live for my son!"

"Then you better go find the smiley face," Zach said.

The screen went black.

Kayce started toward the production floor, with Cooter right behind her. Bonnie shook her head, then looked down at her mother's body.

"Fuck this. Fuck all this."

She pulled the hammer out of her mother's skull and walked toward the door, blood dripping off onto the floor.

As soon as she was gone, I started toward the lobby.

He had to have hidden the damn thing tonight. It was too bright to not be noticed by someone, and if he'd hidden it among the products waiting to be shipped, it could be long gone. I knew he'd been in the building to place his screen and the cameras. That meant the most likely place to find it was in the break room, or the lobby.

Right now, I wanted to be in the room that didn't have three dead bodies in it.

In the lobby, I tried the office door and found it locked. I didn't expect otherwise,

I doubted the company would trust anyone from the night shift in there, but I had to check. Process of elimination.

I walked to the glass doors that led out into the world and stared at my car in the parking lot. Safety, a chance to get away. But some kind of contraption was on the other side of the glass, and I knew if I tried to leave, it would blow.

So instead, I went to the vinyl chairs by the door. Flipping them over, I checked the bottoms, then the backs for any sign of the smiley.

Nothing.

I returned the chairs to where they'd been.

Why are you being clean? Tear the place apart!

But day shift...

Day shift!

There was another shift coming in! I checked my phone. 1:24 AM. They'd be here in three and a half hours. As soon as they saw the devices, they'd call the police and the game would be over.

I just had to survive that long.

And they could clean up the mess.

There was a table with brochures and catalogs across the room, under the company logo. I swept them off the table, watching for the flash of anything metallic. Then I flipped the table, looking, still looking.

The plant between the chairs went next, dumped unceremoniously on the vinyl wood floor. Picking up the plant, I shook it by the roots, but nothing fell out. Using my foot, I kicked through the dirt.

Three more chairs were further back in the lobby, along with a display of the company's products. The chairs went first, overturned and tossed out of the way.

Reaching the display, I started ripping open packaging, throwing bubble wrap and other shit toward the center of the room as I worked. Finally, I reached the last item, a cardboard box full of "premium recycled packaging material." I opened it, rolling out the bubble wrap and finding nothing.

Fuck.

I looked around. Nothing in the lobby had been untouched by my destruction. There was no piece of furniture, no display, that I had missed.

It wasn't here.

That meant the break room.

And three bodies.

With my feet, I cleared a path to the break room door. Tom's body still lay on the other side. For a moment, I thought about dragging him out into the lobby.

Too much work, I decided.

I scanned the room. A counter on one wall, six tables in two rows of three in the center. Chairs, trash cans, it was going to take awhile to go through this one.

Not counting the three bodies.

Had I missed anything in the lobby?

I turned around and looked. The only thing still where it had been when I started was the logo on the wall.

The logo.

It was in relief, jutting out from the wall.

But was it permanently mounted?

I crossed the lobby for a closer look.

There was a crack between the logo and the wall.

Carefully, I put my hands on the bottom and lifted.

It moved.

I grabbed it and hurled it toward the center of the lobby.

There, on the back, a face smiled back at me, duct-taped to the wood. I peeled it off, putting the survival token in my pocket.

From the factory floor, someone screamed.

10

I RAN THROUGH THE break room and onto the factory floor. Bonnie and Kayce were standing by one of the machines, and I went toward them. As I got closer, I saw the body lying on the floor between them.

"Cooter?" I said.

Bonnie nodded. "He tried to rape me."

I knelt next to the body. His throat had been cut, blood pouring out onto the floor around him. A retractable box cutter was lying next to him. I looked up at Bonnie.

"You slit his throat?"

She nodded. "He started it, I finished it."

I looked at Kayce. "Is that what happened?"

She nodded, her hands fidgeting.

"Are you sure?"

"Damn it, Trey," Bonnie cut in. "Of course she's sure. Perv-O here grabbed me and pushed me up against the machine, and I slit his throat. Lucky I had my knife on me from going through packages in shipping."

I nodded. "Just one question."

"What?"

"Which pocket was your knife in?"

"My pants pocket, obviously."

"And where are your pants?"

She looked down at her naked body, covered only by the vest and the elimination device, and shook her head. "You're a moron, Trey. Why the fuck do you care about me killing the man who brutally murdered my mother in front of me?"

"Because it's gone to your head," I said, getting to my feet. "All of this bullshit, you're acting like it's personal, not some stupid fuck messing with us for his amusement!"

"It is personal!" Bonnie yelled back. "My mother is dead. My lover is dead. If that's not personal, I don't know what the fuck is!"

She took a deep breath. "You don't understand. You never understood. I've had a fucking emotional roller coaster tonight. Tom knocked me up. I got an abortion because he promised we could be together in a couple years when he retired, and have all the kids I wanted. Now he's gone, and apparently my own mother was fucking him too? What the fuck?"

Bonnie turned to Kayce. "Were you fucking him too?"

Kayce shook her head. "Not a damn chance."

"I don't know what the fuck I'm feeling," Bonnie said, turning back to me. "But this asshole," she gestured at Cooter's body, "gave me a chance to get some of those emotions out. And I did. So fuck you, Trey, if you think it's too personal or whatever. As far as I'm concerned, you can go to hell. I'm gonna go find that damn smiley face and save my ass!"

She turned and started to walk away, when the speakers cracked to life. "You want to tell her, Trey, or should I?"

Bonnie turned. "Tell me what?"

I reached into my pocket and took out the smiley face. "It was in the lobby."

"Fuck," Kayce whispered.

"Were you going to say something?" Bonnie asked.

"I got a little distracted when I saw this." I gestured to the body on the ground.

Bonnie grabbed the knife off the floor, then turned to face me. "Fuck you, Trey. You broke my heart, and you done showed up on a day with no fucking rules. I'm gonna kill your ass like I wanted to since the day you left, and there ain't gonna be no consequences for it."

I froze. She was right, if she wanted to, she could try to kill me, and I'd have to fight for my life. "Bonnie, please," I held up my hands.

"I like it when you beg, you bastard," she replied, stepping toward me. "It reminds me of how I begged the day you left."

My eyes didn't leave the knife. It was a utility knife, a box cutter, but I knew it was dangerous.

"You want me to beg? I'll beg all you want. I'll get down on my knees if you want me to."

She laughed, actually threw her head back and laughed, and I saw my chance. Stepping forward, I swung my right fist in an uppercut, connecting hard with her jaw.

11

Bonnie's mouth closed, and she fell backward, landing on the concrete floor in a heap.

"Is she dead?" Kayce whispered.

I knelt next to Bonnie and put my fingers to her neck. "No. She's got a pulse. Just unconscious."

"How could you… I mean, I'm sure you wanted to, but…"

"I've got a wife and kid to go home to." I picked up the knife and got to my feet.

Stepping away from Bonnie, I hurled it as far as I could toward the warehouse side.

"I never liked her," Kayce admitted. "First because she was a bitch, then because she thought she was untouchable when Tom was fucking her."

I nodded. "Let's get her into the break room." Bending, I lifted her, then threw her over my shoulder in a fireman's carry.

***

Zach was on the screen when we got there.

"That was one of the most beautiful things I've ever seen!" he said as I lay Bonnie on one of the tables. "Do you know how often I wanted to do that? Just lay the heartless bitch out?"

"Yeah, well, it was self-defense," I said, turning to face the screen. I paused for a moment.

The bodies were gone.

Kayce noticed it too, her mouth open as she turned to look at me.

"What, did you want me to leave those stinkers in there for you to deal with?" Zach asked.

"He's somewhere close," Kayce whispered.

I nodded.

"I'm glad they're gone," I said. "They *were* starting to stink."

"Nice to be appreciated," Zach replied. "Well, we're rapidly running out of time, so let's wake up sleeping beauty and get on to our next activity!"

There was a plastic pitcher on the counter. I filled it with water, and threw it in Bonnie's face.

Her eyes flew open. "What! What the?"

"Good morning," Zach said.

"What happened?" she muttered, rubbing her jaw.

"New Guy decided he wasn't going to let you do him like you did Cooter," Zach said. "So he K.O.'ed you."

"Fuck," she groaned. "He packs a wallop for a pansy-ass."

Zach laughed again. "Well, he's safe for this activity, so don't get any ideas."

"Can't I have some time to recover?" Bonnie asked.

I looked at the clock. 2:38. Someone on day shift would be an early bird, I was sure. That would cut into the time Zach had for the rest of his twisted revenge program.

"Nope!" Zach grinned.

"So what now?" Bonnie asked. "You want us to have a bleach-chugging contest? Maybe turn on the machines and dive head-first into the rollers?"

"I'm not that sadistic," Zach said. "Besides, those would kill both of you. There has to be a winner for the next challenge."

"A winner," Bonnie said. "So what the fuck is the next challenge?"

"That's for me to know and you to find out—if you win." Zach grinned.

"Win what?" Kayce asked. She was standing behind me, next to the counter. Bonnie was closer to the monitor.

"A fight to the death."

"What?" Kayce yelled.

"Kill or be killed. The fight starts now."

Bonnie turned toward Kayce, an evil glint in her eye. "Maybe I'll just go ahead and kill both of you," she snarled.

A foot landed on the table next to me, then I saw Kayce leap off the table onto Bonnie.

She crashed backwards into the table with the monitor, knocking it to the floor. Kayce landed on top of her, her elbow slamming into Bonnie's gut.

Bonnie gasped. "My back," she moaned.

Kayce didn't care. A small knife appeared in her hand, and she slashed one of the straps on Bonnie's vest, next to the elimination device.

Nothing happened.

She cut another.

Nothing happened.

With a yell of frustration, Kayce plunged the knife into Bonnie's throat. Bonnie hadn't moved since she landed on the table.

Had Kayce paralyzed her?

It didn't matter. The blood flowing from the wound in Bonnie's neck would finish her.

Kayce stood up, looking down at Bonnie's body, then at me. "I had to, my kid," she said.

I nodded understanding. "Where'd you get the knife?"

She pointed behind me, and I turned to see an open drawer, some other utensils inside.

Getting to my feet, I went to set up the monitor, but it had been snapped in half at some point during the melee.

"What now?" Kayce asked.

As quickly as I could, I peeled off my vest and put it on top of Bonnie. After a moment, Kayce did the same.

"Do you think he was lying about the doors too?"

I shrugged. "There's no telling."

"Can we try one?"

"I wouldn't."

12

Kayce and I looked around.

"Where'd that come from?" she whispered.

"Back here."

I moved the coffee machine on the counter to find a speaker behind it.

"I'll be honest," Zach's voice came over the speaker. "I figured someone would figure that shit out sooner. I mean, the damn buckles are plastic. That's not conductive."

"But the doors are rigged to blow?" I asked.

"Oh yes. And in case you're thinking of trying something, I still know where your loved ones are." I could hear the pleasure in his voice. "Also, this place is a fucking tinderbox. If my little device in the warehouse goes off, all the cardboard and oil and shit will make this place go up in smoke. That'll leave you with a tough choice: die by smoke inhalation or shrapnel from the doors."

"We're not going to try anything," Kayce said. "Just let us go, and we won't tell anyone."

Laughter. "Five dead bodies and you think you can just keep it a secret? Come on, Kayce. You know better."

She shook her head, a tear coming to her eye.

"Now, we don't have much time left. Both of you, go to the plant manager's office."

She looked at me and I shrugged. "I don't know where that is."

"This way," she said, taking my hand.

For a moment, I wanted to jerk it away—I was married, why did this naked woman think she could touch me? Then I realized it was a comfort, and I thought maybe it was the same for her.

She led me across the lobby, through the mess I'd made, to the office door.

"It was locked earlier," I said.

Kayce tried the handle, and it opened. She looked up at me, confused.

"He's close," I said, pointing down.

A trail of blood led across the lobby to the office door.

"Fuck," she breathed.

"Let me go first," I said.

I followed the blood trail through the front part of the office and down a hall. It turned into a room, and I flipped on the light.

It was a conference room, the four bodies in chairs around the table.

"Fuck, that's creepy." Kayce stepped back toward the door.

"Stinky," I said, smelling the copper twang of blood mixing with the odor of decomposition.

"That's the manager's office," she said, pointing to a cracked door at the end of the hall.

"Right," I said. I crept down the hall. When I got to the end, I pushed the door open.

Nothing happened.

I reached inside and felt the wall until I found the light. I flipped it on.

Nothing happened.

I looked inside.

The office was empty. It was large and spacious, with a massive wooden desk in the center. Bookshelves were behind the desk, mostly displaying photos of an older man and his wife, children, grandchildren, and various awards. At the far end, two massive windows looked out at the highway.

"I bet this guy ain't making eleven dollars an hour," I muttered.

"And you'd be right!" One of the computer monitors turned on, and Zach's face reappeared. "This is what middle class looks like. Six figure job, cushy office, a boat to play with on the weekend, everything you and I can dream of if we just work hard, pull ourselves up by the bootstraps, and kiss the right asses on the way up."

"So what?" I asked. "You want us to take a shit on his desk or something?" I was eyeing the windows. Zach had said the doors were rigged, but had he gotten the windows too?

"You have a sense of humor, New Guy. I like it. But no. A simple crap isn't enough. I spent hours watching the camera in that office, watching the manager fuck anyone he could, the fat secretary, the saggy-tits accountant, the Human Resources manager with enough silicone in her to grease an elephant, even his wife!"

I raised an eyebrow to Kayce, who shrugged. "Management drama."

"I want to see someone get fucked on that desk that's actually good looking. To cleanse my mind of the horrors I've seen take place there. New guy, I hope you're horny, because you're gonna get to fuck Kayce."

13

"I'm married," I protested. "I don't want to cheat on my wife."

On the screen, Zach smiled. "If that's the problem, it's one I can fix…"

"No!" I yelled, stepping toward the desk.

Kayce grabbed my arm. "Please, Trey. I don't want to either, but I don't want anything to happen to my kid." She paused, then looked up at me, moving to press her body against mine. "I need you, Trey."

"That's right, Trey," Zach chimed in. She needs you, her kid needs you, your wife needs you, your kid needs you, there's just a lot of people who need you right now."

Fuck. This was a line I didn't want to cross. Elise was the love of my life, and even with what had already happened tonight, I felt like she would forgive me. But if I fucked another woman, all bets were off, even if it saved all of our lives.

But there were a lot of lives riding on my willingness to fuck Kayce. Both our families, along with whoever else this twisted creep decided to end. I looked down at Kayce and sighed.

"Please," she said, stepping back and holding out her arms, showing me her body.

She was attractive. Kayce had curves in places my wife didn't, large breasts and a nice ass.

"Take your clothes off, New Guy," Zach said. "Let's see what you're working with."

I hesitated for a moment, and Zach shook his head. "Don't make me do it, New Guy."

I hoped Elise would forgive me.

Before I could move, Kayce's hands were on my belt buckle. Undoing it, she unbuttoned my pants and let them fall to the floor. I stepped out of them, then pulled my t-shirt over my head, then dropped my boxers, leaving me in my socks.

I was already hard, even if I'd been trying to hide it.

Kayce dropped to her knees in front of me, taking my cock in her mouth. "Goddamn," she breathed. "I can't wait to get this inside me."

I wanted to stop, to step back, to find Zach and kill him. But Kayce's mouth was so warm, and the way she was moving her tongue, I didn't want her to stop. "Just like that, baby,"

"I want you in me," she whispered. "I want this hard cock in my pussy."

Time for the decision. I had to put everything I had into making this convincing, or stop now and let all of us face the consequences.

It wasn't Elise I thought of then, but Hannah. My little girl deserved a full life, not one cut short by a madman.

"Get on the desk," I growled.

She pushed everything she could off the desk before laying down on it, face up. I stepped up to her, reaching out to grab her breast.

"You like my titties, baby?"

"Oh, I love them," I said, moving to slide my cock into her.

"Trey, be gentle," she said. "I haven't… since Baxter…"

"Really?"

A nod.

I dropped to my knees. Finding her pussy at the perfect height, I slid my tongue between her lips.

"Oh, you devil," Kayce growled as I found her clit and gently sucked, then moved my tongue over it. "Oh, I'm not sure I'm going to let your wife have you back. Sweet lord, that feels amazing."

Without looking up, I took my hand off the floor and slid a pair of fingers into her pussy.

"God, yes!" she gasped. "Don't fucking stop, whatever you do, don't fucking stop."

My angle changed as her back arched off the desk, and the moans turned into screams.

"Oh God, oh God, Trey, I'm coming, don't stop, Trey. Don't fucking stop!"

Finally, I heard her exhale, and her back returned to the desk.

"That was so good, baby," she whispered as I stood up.

I looked over at the monitor. It was black, but I knew Zach was still watching, probably with his hand in his pants.

"Don't think about him, baby," Kayce said. "Just give me that hard, throbbing cock."

"Is that what you need?"

A nod. "Uh huh."

I stepped up to the desk, and she wrapped her legs behind me. Gravity was working against her breasts, flattening them, but they were still sexy as hell. Reaching down, I caressed one, drawing a smile.

"If you fuck me, they'll jiggle," Kayce promised.

I smiled. Kayce was making it easy to forget about my wife, about Zach, about everything but her.

I slid my cock into her, and she inhaled sharply. "Wow."

"You like that?"

She nodded. "Bigger than Baxter."

I put her legs on my shoulders, then began to fuck her hard.

She was right, her breasts did bounce.

Her pussy was incredible. Tight, warm, sending waves of sensation from my cock up through my body. She was so fucking good.

"Harder," she purred. "Harder."

I found a way to get deeper, pushing as far into Kayce as I could.

"Damn," I muttered.

"We're gonna have to do this again," she whispered. "Good God, we're going to have to do this again."

I had no idea how it would happen, but I wanted it. Guilt rose, but I pushed it down. "Oh fuck, yes baby. I want to do this again."

"Oh God." I felt her pussy start to tighten around my cock.

"I'm close,"

"Fill me, baby, Give it all to me."

She closed her eyes, just lying there, whimpering, and I knew she was coming again.

That sent me over the edge, and I shot my load deep inside her.

14

I looked down at Kayce, lying naked on the desk, my cock still in her.

"Thank you," she whispered.

"You okay?" I asked, offering a hand to help her up.

Kayce nodded. "I've just never been fucked like that." She smiled. "I kind of want to ask him to make you a widower."

"Really?"

Zach's voice broke the moment and brought us back to reality. "No!" we yelled together, and he laughed.

"You have no idea how many times I watched someone get fucked on that desk from my office down here. But that was by far the best. I'm glad I recorded it."

Kayce blushed.

"You did what?" I asked.

"Do you want a copy too?" Zach asked. "I'm glad to send it to you, let me just… oops, that was your wife's email."

I looked over at the screen to see him grinning. I wanted to reach through the screen and grab him, to hurl him out one of the office's windows onto the highway, where a series of eighteen wheelers would run him over.

Then something hit me.

Down here.

"He's in the basement," I whispered to Kayce.

I walked toward the office door.

"Where are you going?" Zach asked from the monitor.

In the hall, I found three of the doors were closed. I tried the first one.

It swung open. I reached in and turned on the light to reveal an office.

I passed the conference room and looked inside. Bonnie's body was in there now, next to her mother.

Fuck me, I was right.

The next empty door opened to reveal another office.

The final one had a small placard on it. *Stairs.*

I opened it a crack, and saw steps leading down. At the bottom, lights were on.

Bingo.

I closed the door again, and stepped out into the main office. There was a desk nearby, and I pulled it toward the hall. It was a heavy motherfucker—wide too, I could barely get it into the hallway—but finally it was parked in front of the door to the stairs, blocking it.

Let's see that fucker get out now.

I walked back to the manager's office to find Kayce looking confused, and Zach grinning.

"You feel better now?" he asked.

"Yeah." I said. "I do feel better."

"Good." He smiled.

An explosion rocked the building.

Kayce stumbled, falling into my arms.

Zach typed something, and I heard another explosion, this one from the warehouse.

"I'm gonna burn this place to the ground!" he yelled as the screen went black. "Fuck this place!" We heard a gunshot, then nothing.

"What do we do?" Kayce asked.

"Come on."

We scrambled out into the hall, climbing over the desk, and pushing open the lobby door.

A wave of heat hit us. The shit I'd scattered all over the lobby was burning, ignited by someone trying to come in the front door.

The first explosion.

Zach had caused the second.

"Fuck, go back," I said, pushing Kayce away from the door.

The outer office had floor to ceiling windows too, and I grabbed one of the chairs.

"Stand back!" I said, winding up and swinging the chair into the window.

It bounced off, barely scratching it.

"Fuck!" I ran toward the hall and jumped over the desk. In the manager's office, I found what I was looking for, a heavy rock bookend.

"Hurry!" Kayce said, appearing in the door.

I ran to one of the windows and started slamming the bookend against it. Three times, four, then it finally cracked.

I pulled my arm back, then smashed the rock into the window again.

It shattered.

Kayce jumped through, with me right behind her, and we ran to the parking lot. Smoke was curling into the sky, Zach had made a good start on burning the place to the ground.

I looked at Kayce, naked, wide-eyed, and worried, then down at my own naked body. In the distance, I heard the first sirens approaching.

"Are you okay?" I asked.

She nodded. "We made it. We fucking made it."

Epilogue

The bell over the door jingled as I entered the service station on Route 209.

"Hey, it's the rich man," Eddie greeted me.

I couldn't help but smile. After what happened, the company had given Kayce and me enough money to live comfortably for the rest of our lives and then some.

"I ain't that rich," I said, picking out a candy bar. "That money's gotta last me a long time."

Eddie nodded. "I'm glad you understand that. I've seen too many folks who would just blow through the money and wonder where it went."

I shook my head. "Ain't no reason to do that."

He nodded. "Elise come home yet?"

I shook my head. Zach had sent the damn video of me and Kayce to my wife. She'd left, gone to her mothers to think things over. It took almost two months to convince her that it had been nothing but survival, and everything I'd done had been with the intention to get back to her.

The first night she was back at home, Kayce called to tell me she was pregnant.

The next morning, Elise left again.

"Give it time," Eddie said. "I know you went through a lot, and she'll come around."

I took a deep breath and nodded. "Yeah. Maybe."

He looked at me for a moment, then shook his head. "That was a hell of a mess you found yourself in."

I nodded agreement.

The phone rang, distracting Eddie.

"Hello?" He held it out. "It's for you."

I took it. "Hello?"

"Hi there, New Guy."

I froze. "You're dead." The sheriff had assured me of it, explaining how they found a body with a bullet hole through the skull in the basement server room. Blood type had matched Zach. It was him.

A laugh. "Hell ain't got a long distance connection! Sheriff Peters took the first solution that fit what was in front of him, and boy, was he wrong. I'm as alive as you are."

"What do you want?" I asked, moving toward the door. He had to be watching.

"I ain't out there, New Guy. Eddie ain't updated his network security. Getting in was easy."

I looked up at the camera in the corner and flipped it the bird.

Zach laughed again. "I hear congratulations are in order. It's nice to think that my little game brought you and Kayce together."

"Funny, I'd love to rip you apart," I growled.

More laughter. "I think I'm safe for now, New Guy. But keep an eye out. I had so much fun during our first game, I might decide to play another…"

I hurled the phone across the store, hitting a glass coffee pot. It shattered, sending brown liquid cascading off the counter to the floor. Eddie looked at the mess, then at me, confused.

"It's over!" I yelled at the camera in the corner, marching toward it. "It's fucking over!" I sank to the floor and buried my face in my hands. "I don't wanna play again."

Acknowledgements

THANK YOU TO:

CHLOE YORK for her editing expertise. She took a book I thought was pretty good and helped me make it better than I could have hoped.

Christy Aldridge with Grim Poppy Designs for the amazing cover.

Wednesday for doing her best to add typos to the manuscript.

Atlas for staying out of the way and watching YouTube.

Anna for all the love.

And you, dear reader, for reading this work!

About the author

D.L. WINCHESTER LIVES IN the foothills of southern Appalachia. A former mortician, his work searches the darkness to find tales worth telling. He is the author of over three hundred obituaries, numerous short stories, the novellas The Screaming House *and* Devil's Fork, *several novelettes, and the collections* Shadows of Appalachia *and* A Terrible Place and Other Flashes of Horror.

D.L. also serves as the President and Associate Editor of Undertaker Books, an independent horror publisher. In his spare time, he can be found searching for inspiration in the world around him and helping his wife try to keep their children from becoming the next generation of horror villains.

Follow the Author

Facebook: https://www.facebook.com/writerdlwinchester

Instagram: https://www.instagram.com/writerdlwinchester

Undertaker Books: https://www.undertakerbooks.com

Also by D.L. Winchester

Shadows of Appalachia
A Terrible Place
The Screaming House
Devil's Fork
Dead Money
The Colony
Mother Clucker
Night of the Chupacabra
It Came From the Morgue
Night Shift

*Return of the Mother Clucker
Rodeo Clown*

www.ingramcontent.com/pod-product-compliance
Lightning Source LLC
LaVergne TN
LVHW020450070526
838199LV00063B/4901